Wild Horse Run

Suzanne Weyn

PRICE STERN SLOAN
Los Angeles

For Nancy Krulik
with much thanks

Published by Price Stern Sloan, Inc.
11150 Olympic Boulevard
Los Angeles, California 90064
ISBN: 0-8431-3617-0
Printed in the United States of America

10 9 8 7 6 5 4 3 2 1

Contents

1. Welcome to Camp Lakewood...................4

2. Windswept 11

3. Missing!.................................16

4. Making Friends 22

5. On the Run 28

6. Lara's Horse............................35

7. Jumping 40

8. Let's Go, Lara! 46

9. The Good Luck Hat 53

10. And the Winner Is 58

Welcome to Camp Lakewood

Barbie turned her red convertible onto the long dirt road leading to Camp Lakewood. The horse trailer attached to a hookup on the back bumper forced her to go extra slowly.

"Midge must be so excited," said Barbie's friend Kira, who sat beside her. "Opening this camp for underprivileged girls is her dream come true."

Christie leaned forward from the back seat. "Isn't it funny to think that when Midge inherited this property everyone called it The Haunted Mansion? We sure had our hands full when we helped her fix it up."

Barbie looked ahead at the large white house, gleaming in the summer sunlight.

"It's gorgeous now," said Skipper from the back seat.

As Barbie pulled up in front of the house, Midge stepped out onto the front porch to greet them. She was dressed in jeans and a plaid shirt. "Hi, guys!"

"Midge, the place looks fantastic," said Barbie, getting out of the car.

"Thanks to you guys and all your help," Midge replied. Barbie and the gang all helped Midge turn the tumbledown house and its overgrown property into a camp. But Barbie hadn't seen it since Midge and her husband Alan had added the finishing touches.

Kira grabbed her camera and snapped a quick picture of Barbie and Midge standing on the porch. "I've got to keep in practice if I'm going to run the photography shed," she said with a smile.

Christie took a pair of roller skates from the back seat. "I got Lambert's Sports Store to donate five pairs," she said.

"That's great!" cried Midge happily.

Barbie opened the horse trailer and led her beautiful palomino horse over to a patch of grass under a tree. "Isn't it beautiful here?" she spoke fondly to Stomper.

At that moment Barbie's boyfriend, Ken, stepped out onto the porch.

Barbie smiled at him. "Hi!"

"It's a good thing Ken got here a week early to help us do last-minute repairs," said Midge. "He's been a huge help. Alan and I really appreciate it, Ken."

"It's been fun," Ken said, smiling.

"Come on," said Midge. "I'll give you a tour." She led the gang over the grass-covered hills until they came to a group of large wooden cabins. "That's Cabin Two, Skipper," Midge said. "The twelve-year-olds are in there. You'll be the junior counselor for that cabin."

"Let's get you set up in there," said Barbie. Skipper nodded and flipped her long, blond

French braid over one shoulder. She and Barbie were about to go in when they heard two voices arguing inside the cabin.

"Now, Lara, please!" an older voice was saying. "I promised your mother that there would be no trouble if you spent the summer here at Camp Lakewood."

A young girl answered her. "I don't belong in this nerdy camp. My mother just sent me here so she wouldn't have to bother with me."

Just then, the older woman noticed Skipper and Barbie standing behind the screen door. "Barbie! Skipper!" the woman cried.

"It's good to see you, Amy," said Barbie. Amy was the camp administrator. She also took care of the place during the winter months.

"This is my god-daughter, Lara," Amy told Barbie and Skipper. "Lara, Skipper will be in charge of this cabin and Barbie will be the horseback riding instructor."

"Horseback, huh," said Lara, who was a thin girl of twelve with chin-length brown hair and a line of freckles across her nose. "Could you teach me to ride really well?"

"I think you can learn anything you put your mind to," said Barbie. "If you really want to learn, I can teach you."

"Cool," said Lara.

At that moment, a group of girls came bounding into the cabin with beach towels wrapped around their bathing suits. "Too bad you missed the swim, Lara," said a girl. "Alan is teaching us to dive."

"It's not too bad to me," Lara replied gruffly. "My brain might have gotten as water-logged as yours."

"Lara," Amy said in a warning voice.

Midge opened the door and looked in. "Girls, get showered and then come down for lunch."

Skipper threw her flowered canvas suitcase on an empty bed. "I'll make sure they're all there, Midge. You guys can go on without me."

Barbie followed Midge as she gave them the tour of the rest of the camp. There was a waterfront area, a stable with a riding ring, an archery range, a photography shed, an arts and crafts room, and even a small stage for shows. "You'll be staying in the main house," Midge told Barbie, Christie and Kira.

"I'd better get back and bring Stomper down to the stable," Barbie said. "I can't wait to work with the girls."

"I'm looking forward to it, too," said Midge with a smile. "But I'm afraid you'll have your work cut out for you with Lara. I think we all will."

2

Windswept

Later that night, after the lights were out, the gang gathered on the couches around the fireplace in the main house. "I want to talk to you about something, Barbie," said Midge. "Two weeks from now there will be a horse competition in town for girls under eighteen. There's a big prize for the winning team. The camp could sure use that money. Without it, I might have to sell the horses by next year."

"Do you want me to find some campers who can ride, and work with them?" Barbie asked.

"Do you think you could?" Midge asked hopefully.

"I'll give it my best try," said Barbie.

Suddenly, a loud thud came from the porch. Then they heard a man's voice cry out in pain!

In a second the whole gang was out on the porch. There they saw Alan lying on the porch clutching his ankle. "I tripped on that skateboard," he said, wincing in pain.

"That's Lara's," Amy said apologetically. "I told her to move it. That girl just doesn't listen sometimes."

Alan started to get up, but he stumbled. "I don't think I can put weight on it."

"Come on," said Ken. "I'll run you into town to see a doctor."

"I'll go with you," said Midge.

After Midge, Alan and Ken left, Barbie and the others went inside. "That Lara!" Amy fumed. "She's her own worst enemy."

"What do you mean?" Barbie asked.

"People try to be good to her, but she just makes trouble," said Amy. "Lara is high-spirited, but that's not really the problem."

"What do you think it is?" Christie asked.

"Lara's father died two years ago," Amy explained. "Her mother never quite got over it. She's been a bit distant since then, almost as if she's in a dream world. In a way, Lara lost both her father and her mother at the same time."

"How sad," said Kira.

"It is," Amy agreed. "For the last two years, Lara has been one angry girl."

Two hours later, Alan hobbled in on crutches with his foot in a boot. "It's a bad sprain," Ken reported, coming in behind him. "He'll have to stay off it for a while."

The next morning in the main dining room, Barbie noticed that Skipper looked tired.

"I'm exhausted," Skipper grumbled. "That Lara! She picked on a nice, shy girl named Susan Laine," Skipper continued. "Then she played her radio all night under her covers and when I told her to turn it off, she said, 'It's a free country,' and wouldn't. She has the worst attitude I've ever seen."

Barbie put a comforting hand on Skipper's shoulder. "Hang in there, Sis. Maybe with tender-loving care, Lara will come around."

Just then, Midge came in. "I'm off to a horse auction," she reported. "You're in charge. I hope everything stays calm."

"It will," Barbie assured her.

Barbie had a little free time after breakfast, so she rode Stomper all around the camp grounds. It felt good to be riding again. Before coming to camp, Barbie had been in Hollywood making a movie. The busy schedule hadn't left her much time for riding.

Eventually the path led her back to the main house. As she emerged from the trees, Barbie saw Midge's black sports car. Barbie rode up to the car and gently pulled the horse to a stop.

"Wait until you see the gorgeous horse we bought," said Midge excitedly "He was so inexpensive I couldn't resist. His name is Windswept, and he's beautiful!"

Kira and her nature photography group stepped out of a nearby wooded area. "We're just in time to get a picture of this great new horse," she said with a smile.

Barbie dismounted and opened the horse trailer. Kira and her group stood by watching. "Stand back," Barbie warned them as she took hold of the black horse's reins and led him out. "A horse can be skittish in new surroundings."

Just then, Lara walked by. Grabbing up a garden hose she called out, "Hey, Kira, get a load of this!" With that she sprayed water right at Susan Laine, who was in Kira's group.

Susan screamed and tried to jump out of the way. Blinded by the water in her face, she tripped over a tree stump, falling to the ground in Windswept's path.

With a mad shriek of surprise, Windswept broke loose from Barbie's grip and reared up dangerously above the terrified girl!

3

Missing!

Without a thought for her own safety, Barbie dove in front of the angry horse. Quickly, she grabbed Susan and pulled her out of his path.

"Are you all right?" she asked Susan.

Looking shocked, the girl nodded. "I'm fine. Just scared."

Barbie then turned her attention back to Windswept. "Whoa," she said in a quiet, soothing voice. Slowly, she reached up and took hold of the horse's reins. Right away, Windswept lowered his front legs. Barbie gently stroked his jet-black coat.

"Thanks, Barbie," Midge said, giving her best friend a hug. Then Midge turned to Lara. "As for you, young lady," she said angrily, "do you realize what harm that prank might have caused if Barbie hadn't been here?"

Lara kicked at the dust with her sneaker. "How was I supposed to know the horse was going to go crazy?"

"Barbie, are you OK?" asked Ken, running up to them. "I heard all the commotion."

"I'm fine," said Barbie. "The horse just got scared. He's in a new place, so he's excitable. I'd better get him down to the stables."

Once Windswept was settled in his stall, Barbie made her way back to the mess hall, she could almost taste the tomato soup and tuna fish sandwich she knew was on the day's menu.

After lunch, the camp had an official rest hour—a time for the kids to read, nap or write letters home. Barbie spent the hour saddling up the horses for her first riding class .

At two o'clock, five excited girls came bounding down the hill and into the stables.

"Hi, Barbie," said one of the girls. "Are we going for a long ride today?"

"Not today," Barbie said with a smile. "Riding a horse isn't as easy as it looks. There are some basic skills you have to learn before you can go out on the trail." Barbie looked at the disappointed faces before her. "But I promise you'll all be riding soon," she assured them. "Now, everyone put on a helmet and choose a horse you think you'll like. Let's leave Windswept alone for today," she said.

For the next hour, Barbie taught the kids the proper way to mount a horse, and how to guide by pulling on the reins. By the end of the hour, the kids were steady enough on horseback to follow Barbie as she and Stomper led them on a slow walk around the stables. At the end of the lesson, the kids led their horses back to their stalls.

"I bet these horses aren't the only ones who are hot and tired," Barbie said cheerily. "Does anyone want to join me for a cool dip in the lake? Go change into your suits and meet me at the waterfront dock. But nobody goes in the water until I get there. OK?"

While the kids went back to their cabins to change, Barbie went to the main house and put on a shimmering one-piece bathing suit of yellow, pink, purple and blue.

When she arrived at the lake, Barbie saw Ken out in the water teaching his canoeing class. She watched as Ken helped the kids paddle their canoes into a circle.

Suddenly someone let out a wild "Whoop!" One of the canoes tipped over and the two campers inside went tumbling into the water.

Immediately, Ken jumped out of his canoe and swam over to the capsized canoe. There, swimming happily, was a laughing Lara. Not so happy was the girl who had been in the canoe with her.

"She flipped it on purpose," the girl complained, treading water.

"I was hot, all right?" Lara shouted.

Barbie saw that Ken was working hard to keep calm. "Lara, swim over to the dock, please," he said as he leaned his weight onto the canoe and righted it. Then he helped the other camper back in and got into the back of the canoe himself.

"Lara, why did you do that?" Barbie asked as Lara pulled herself onto the dock.

"For fun!" Lara said angrily. "No one knows what that is around here!"

That night, the whole camp gathered around a blazing campfire. With the help of the counselors, the kids toasted marshmallows. Alan brought out his guitar, and everyone sang. Then it was time for a ghost story.

"I've heard that there was once a ghost who lived in these very woods," Kira began in a spooky voice. "He was the ghost of a pioneer who was lost during a terrible storm… "

Barbie smiled. No one could tell a scary story like Kira. Even Lara would have to enjoy one of Kira's stories. But, as Barbie searched the group around the campfire for Lara, she couldn't find her!

Getting up quietly, Barbie turned on her flashlight and followed the path to Lara's cabin. But Lara wasn't there. Barbie checked the main house. Still no Lara. Quickly, Barbie ran back to the campfire. "Midge," she said, quietly taking her friend aside. "I can't find Lara. I think she may have run away."

4

MAKING FRIENDS

"OK everyone," said Barbie. "This is the plan. Skipper, you assemble all the kids in the main house and keep them calm. Christie, check the arts and crafts shed. Kira, you check the photography shed. Alan, stay here and make sure the campfire is out. Midge, you'd better check the stables, Lara seemed interested in horses, maybe she's there. Ken and I will take the car and check the roads leading from camp."

With that, the search parties split up. Barbie and Ken took off in the convertible. They drove slowly down the long, dark road that ran from camp into town. Barbie spotted a lone figure walking along the side of the road. "Ken, I think that's her," Barbie said.

"Let's go get her," said Ken.

But Barbie didn't speed up. She was afraid Lara might get frightened and run into the woods. Gently, she eased the car up beside the girl. Then she stopped. "Hi, Lara," she said.

"Go away," Lara snapped. "I'm not going back to camp. You're wasting your time."

Lara began to run, but Barbie got out of the car and caught up to her. "Amy will be so upset if you go," she told the girl. "She's told your mother she'd keep an eye on you."

"Amy doesn't care what happens to me. Neither does my mother," Lara said angrily.

"I don't think that's true," Barbie disagreed. "Besides, there's someone else who cares what happens to you. Me."

Lara didn't say anything, but her expression softened. Barbie put her arm around the girl's shoulder. "Come on, Lara, come back to camp. It's not all that bad."

"Well, I am kind of tired," said Lara sulkily.

When they arrived back at camp, Midge ran down the steps of the main house.

"She's had a rough night," Barbie said, seeing the anger on Midge's face.

"So have I," said Midge heatedly. "Lara, Amy is frantic! As of right now, you are docked from all regular camp activities for two days!"

Barbie looked at Midge. A punishment like that was just the thing that would make Lara run away again. "Regular camp activities, huh?" Barbie said softly. "Well, that doesn't mean you can't do some irregular camp activities. What if Lara helps me down at the stables, Midge?"

Midge frowned thoughtfully. "I guess that would be all right. I don't want to make you miserable, Lara. But you have to cooperate."

Lara nodded at Midge then looked down at her feet. "Thanks, Barbie," she whispered.

Barbie smiled. She suspected it wasn't easy for a tough kid like Lara to say thanks.

The next morning after breakfast, Lara met Barbie in the stables. "Hi," Barbie greeted her as she handed Lara a horse brush. "We have a busy day ahead of us. Please comb Stomper while I get the other horses saddled," she said.

"The only thing not stupid about this camp is the horses," Lara said as she brushed. "They have better horses here than at the last camp I went to."

"Where was that?" Barbie asked.

"A couple of years ago, I went to Camp Kendale. That was the year my father...well, it was two years ago. They had horses there, too, but they were all really old."

"Come on outside," she said to Lara. "Let's see what you can do."

Smiling, Lara followed Barbie to the horse ring. She mounted easily and took the horse around the ring, first at a trot and then a canter. In a few minutes, she brought the horse to a stop and dismounted. "You're good," Barbie told her. "Did you learn at camp?"

"Yeah," said Lara. "I liked riding, but I didn't like the head counselor. I had a few run-ins with her and was sent home."

When Barbie and Lara returned to the stable, Windswept snorted restlessly. "I'd better walk him," Barbie said.

Barbie saddled the horse and led him out.

As she entered the ring, a group of girls came running down the hill with Midge. It was time for their riding lesson. Barbie left Windswept in the ring and went back to help the kids get their horses ready. As she did, she noticed that Cindy, a red-headed girl of eight, was running toward Windswept. "I want him," she shouted.

"Cindy, no!" Barbie called as she started running toward the girl.

But Cindy was fast and had ridden horses before. She quickly mounted Windswept, enraging him. He reared back on his mighty hind legs and whinnied angrily. Cindy screamed in horror as he tossed her into the air.

Free of his rider, Windswept ran to the stable fence and jumped to freedom!

5

On the Run

With lightning speed, Barbie ran to the haystack where the girl had landed. "Are you OK?" Barbie asked the shaking girl.

Slowly, Cindy nodded, yes. "Gosh, were you lucky to have fallen in this haystack," Barbie said as she helped her onto her feet.

Midge and Lara came running up behind Barbie. "How is she?" asked Midge.

"Bruised and scared but nothing is broken," said Barbie, picking hay from the girl's red hair. "Tomorrow she should come down and I'll get her a gentle horse for a short ride. The best thing to do when you've been thrown is get right back on. But right now, I think she should go to the infirmary and get checked out."

Midge led the girl away as Kira came running down the path. "I heard screams," she said. "Is everything OK?"

Barbie quickly explained what had happened. She asked Kira to take the other campers on a photography walk. Right now, Barbie had to go find Windswept.

With Lara's help, Barbie saddled Stomper and got on. "Come on, Lara," she said. "I'll need your help."

Lara looked up in surprise. Barbie held out her hand. "Hop on," she said. Lara climbed on behind Barbie and they rode out in search of Windswept. For a while they saw no sign of Windswept. Then Lara cried out, "There he is, over by the trees!"

The horse was grazing on some grass near the edge of the woods. When Lara shouted, he looked up and bolted across a field.

"Sorry," said Lara. "I guess I should have been quieter."

"That's OK," Barbie assured her. "We'll find him again. Stay calm when we do, OK?"

As she spoke, Barbie spotted the horse's dark coat in the distance. Windswept was running at top speed, right in the direction of a main road. Barbie hoped he wouldn't run out in front of a car.

As they closed in on Windswept, the horse slowed down. Barbie was bewildered by this until she realized that the horse had stopped for a drink by a narrow stream.

Immediately, Barbie slowed her pace and then brought Stomper to a halt. She and Lara quietly got off the horse. Lara followed Barbie as she silently approached Windswept.

When they were close, the horse sensed their presence and turned. Barbie was sure he was about to bolt once again. But suddenly, Lara stepped ahead of her. "Whoa, boy," she spoke calmly. "Don't run. It's OK. We won't hurt you."

Windswept backed up with a nervous whinny, but he didn't run. Soon Lara was close enough to pet his black mane. "Shhhhh," Lara soothed the horse. "You don't have to be afraid. I know how you feel. I'm just like you. Whenever I get afraid I run away, too. But you can trust me. How about coming back to camp with me?" With that, Lara put her foot into the stirrup and climbed on. Barbie breathed in sharply as the horse bucked, but Lara held on tightly.

To Barbie's surprise, Windswept began to calm down. "Can you ride him over to Stomper?" she asked Lara.

"I think so," Lara answered nervously.

"Take it very slowly," Barbie coached. "Hold the reins tight. If they're too loose, he might take it as a signal to run."

Lara was able to trot Windswept over to Stomper. Barbie mounted her horse, and together they trotted back to the stable. When they were near, the sight of his stall made Windswept balk. He shuffled and snorted, but Lara didn't seem afraid. "It's OK, boy," she said. "You'll be all right there. I'll get you some water and then I'll brush you down. How does that sound, buddy?"

Barbie was amazed. It was as if Windswept understood Lara's words. Instantly, he settled down and continued on to the stable.

In the stable, Barbie smiled as she watched Lara brush Windswept. Even if he was a horse, it was good that Lara had finally made a friend.

After they finished grooming the rest of the horses, Barbie went back to the main house where she showered and changed into shorts and a T-shirt. She came down the stairs in time to hear Midge talking on the phone in the main room. "A deal doesn't count if you don't tell the truth," she was saying to the person on the other end. There was silence as she listened to that person speak. "I don't think you're being very honest," she said with forced calm. "Good-bye."

"What was that about?" Barbie asked.

"I called Windswept's former owner," Midge explained. "It seems he forgot to tell me that he'd bought the horse for his daughter, but she couldn't handle him. Neither could her riding instructor. Well, neither can we! That horse has already endangered two of my campers." Midge sat on a couch and sighed. "I might have to disband the entire program next year if I run out of money. I was really hoping that you could find good riders to win that horse show. But I can't count on that. And with money being so tight, I can't afford to keep a horse that no one can ride."

"I know someone who can ride him," Barbie said with a smile.

6

Lara's Horse

"OK, Barbie," Midge said after an hour-long discussion about Windswept and Lara. "You win. But I'm telling you, Lara is no one to pin your hopes on. This time your magic might not work."

"I'm not counting on magic," Barbie assured her friend. "I'm counting on hard work. Lara, Windswept and I will give it our all. I think we can do it."

"I hope you're right," said Midge skeptically. "Thanks to you, Windswept has until the end of camp to shape up."

Barbie decided to wait until the next morning to tell Lara the good news. Right after breakfast, she hurried down to the stable. But before she got there, she knew someone other than Lara was already there.

She looked in the stable. It appeared to be empty, but Barbie knew differently. "Ken, where are you?" she called.

Ken popped out from behind Stomper's stall. "I wanted to surprise you. How did you know I was here?"

"Your boots gave you away," Barbie laughed, pointing to the dirt. "Look." Ken's boots had left a trail of capital K's in the dirt. The K was printed on the bottom of his boot. Right next to the K's were big B's from the bottom of Barbie's boots.

"K and B," said Ken as he put his arm around Barbie. "They look good together."

"What's *he* doing here?" snapped Lara as she arrived at the stable.

"I was just leaving," Ken said pleasantly. "See ya later."

"Lara, you didn't have to be so rude to Ken," Barbie said gently.

"Why not?" she questioned. "Nobody around here likes me except you and Windswept."

Barbie sighed. "That's not so, Lara. You have to give people a chance."

"No one gives me a chance," Lara insisted.

"Midge is giving you a chance," said Barbie. "A chance to save Windswept."

Lara's eyes went wide. "Save him! Do you mean she wants to get rid of him?"

"Well, yes...and no," Barbie said. "Midge thinks the horse will never be cooperative. But I told her one person might be able to bring Windswept around."

"Me, right?" Lara asked eagerly.

Barbie laughed fondly. "You've got it. But it will take a lot of work. You'll have to spend most of your days with him. Is that OK with you?"

"You bet it's OK! I'd do anything to help Windswept!" Lara said happily. "Windswept and I understand one another, don't we, boy?"

Just then, there was a knock at the open door. It was Susan Laine. "What do you want?" Lara snapped at her.

Susan looked shyly at Lara. "I...um...I was wondering if you could show me your horse."

"*My* horse?" Lara asked in surprise.

"Yes, you know, the one you saved yesterday."

A look of pride came over Lara's face. "Sure, this is him right here."

"Can I pet him?" Susan asked.

Barbie interrupted. "Windswept is a little skittish around strangers, Susan. Maybe you should pet a different horse."

"Windswept will be all right as long as I'm around," Lara insisted. "Pet him behind the ears. He likes that a lot."

"Well, all right," Barbie gave in.

Timidly, Susan climbed onto a stool and gently patted the horse behind his ears.

"I didn't know you liked horses, Susan," Barbie said.

"I love horses. I can ride, too," said Susan.

"I thought you were a city kid like me," said Lara. "Where did you learn to ride?"

"At a Fresh Air Fund Camp. You know, a camp where city kids go for a week or two."

The sound of their laughter made Barbie look over at the girls. It was wonderful to see Lara talking to another camper—especially Susan, to whom Lara had been so unkind.

Susan helped Lara brush Windswept. Then she watched as Lara expertly rubbed a soft cloth all over the horse's body. "You sure know a lot about horses," Susan commented. "Could you teach me what you know?"

Lara looked startled. "Learn from me? Well, maybe...I suppose so. Barbie and I promised Midge we would train Windswept. It's really more than a two-person job, isn't it, Barbie?"

Barbie nodded.

"Would you like to help me train my horse?" Lara asked Susan.

"More than anything!" Susan replied. Barbie smiled as the two girls shook hands.

7

Jumping

That night, Barbie sat with Skipper on the front porch of cabin two. "How are you enjoying being a junior counselor?" Barbie asked.

"I love it," said Skipper, "especially now that Lara isn't as much trouble. Look at her in there. She's actually talking to another camper like a regular kid."

Barbie angled herself just a bit so she could see into the cabin through the window behind her. Lara and Susan were sitting quietly on Lara's bed by the window. Although it was after lights out, they had a small flashlight on and were whispering. "Do you think I should tell them to go to sleep?" Skipper asked Barbie.

"I'd say yes if they were keeping the other campers awake. But everyone else seems to be asleep. Let them talk a few minutes more."

In the quiet, Susan and Lara's voices drifted out onto the porch. "Nobody understands Windswept the way I do," Lara was saying. "He puts on a good show, that's all. He figures if everyone is afraid of him, then no one will bother him. If no one bothers him, then no one can hurt him. But he doesn't have to put on a show for me."

Barbie and Skipper let them talk a half-hour more. "I guess those two had better get some shut-eye," Barbie said finally. "They have a busy day tomorrow."

"Good-night, Sis," said Skipper, getting up. "See you in the morning."

Early the next morning, Barbie's voice rang out over the public address system. "Rise and shine, Camp Lakewood! Up and at 'em! Breakfast will be served in twenty minutes."

She turned away from the microphone toward Skipper, who sat beside her. "That should get them going."

"I know someone who's already up and at 'em," said Skipper. "Lara leapt out of bed this morning, made her bed, and even swept the front porch, which was her chore assignment."

Barbie laughed. "I promised to teach her to jump today. I guess she's excited."

"That's putting it mildly," said Skipper.

After breakfast, Barbie went straight to the stables to run Stomper. She and Stomper were just returning when she met Lara. "I'm ready," said Lara.

"Great," said Barbie. "Let's get started."

"Hey," said Lara. "Look at this trail of stars in the dirt."

"Those are made by Stomper's horseshoes," Barbie explained as she dismounted. "I had them made especially for her."

"Totally cool," said Lara, following Barbie into the stable. Barbie placed a bridle on Windswept. Then she took hold of the horse's reins and led him into the field.

Barbie then got busy setting up rails for Lara to jump. Each rail was higher than the next, but none was very high. "These are so small," Lara complained. "I thought we were going to jump over high hurdles like riders in the Olympics."

"Jumping isn't as easy as it looks," Barbie explained. "Let's start out slowly."

Lara nodded, looking disappointed. As she climbed onto Windswept's back, the horse snorted and backed up. To Barbie, it seemed that both the horse and his rider were nervous about jumping. After a few minutes, though, Windswept calmed down.

"Lara, maybe you should try some exercises first," Barbie suggested. "Just to relax."

"OK," Lara agreed. One by one Barbie explained the exercises. She had Lara sit in the saddle and touch her toes. Then she told her to lean all the way back onto Windswept's back. Finally, Barbie had Lara sit up tall with her arms straight out to her side, turning back and forth in the saddle.

When the exercises were done, Barbie asked, "Ready for your first lesson?"

"Ready as I'll ever be," Lara answered with an anxious smile.

"Watch me," said Barbie. She and Stomper walked slowly over to the first hurdle. It wasn't more than a foot off the ground. Stomper stepped over it gracefully. "Now it's your turn," said Barbie to Lara.

Lara and Windswept managed the first hurdle. The next one was also no problem. But on the third and highest hurdle, Windswept knocked the rail off its posts. "Darn," cried Lara.

"Don't worry," came a girl's voice. It was Susan. "You'll get it next time. It took me a while to learn, too."

"You can jump?" Lara asked.

"A little," Susan answered.

"Go saddle up Clover," Barbie told her. "You can do some jumps with us."

"Great," said Susan, running back to the stable. In minutes, she returned with the gentle, brown and white horse. As she approached, she speeded up and jumped the third hurdle easily.

Spurred by Susan and Clover's example, Lara kicked Windswept lightly on the side, and set off for the hurdle. This time, Windswept jumped it cleanly. "Way to go!" cried Susan.

Barbie watched the girls and smiled. She had come to a decision.

"Girls, come here, please," Barbie called to them. Susan and Lara rode their horses to her. "There is a big riding competition in town in less than two weeks. I'd like you two to represent Camp Lakewood."

"All right!" Susan and Lara cheered.

8

Let's Go, Lara!

For the next week and a half, Lara and Susan practiced jumping. Other campers went to arts and crafts, boating, dramatics, but not Lara and Susan. In fact, sometimes Barbie had to remind them to eat and sleep.

On the night before the big competition, Barbie went to the stable to make sure the horses were bedded down for the night. By the hazy light of sunset, Barbie was shocked to see Lara still jumping Windswept over hurdles. "Lara," she called. Lara turned and rode over to Barbie. "Tonight is the big camp costume party. Why don't you go and have fun with everyone else?" Barbie suggested.

Lara shook her head. "I think we still need some work on that last jump."

"What Windswept needs is some rest, and so do you," Barbie disagreed. "Come to the social, OK? It will be fun."

"I don't have a costume," said Lara.

"We'll whip something up for you," said Barbie.

Reluctantly, Lara gave in. Together they went up to the main house where Barbie lent Lara an orange evening dress and a butterfly mask she'd brought especially for the camp play. Barbie herself dressed in a special pink mermaid costume she'd brought along, knowing there would be a costume party.

When they got to the rec hall, it seemed quiet. "Are you sure this is the place?" Lara asked doubtfully.

"This is the place," said Barbie. She pushed open the door and led Lara into the dark room.

In seconds, the room was a blaze of light.

"Surprise!" the campers and counselors yelled.

Lara jumped back. "A party? For me?"

"And for Susan," Midge said, smiling. "We wanted to wish our star riders good luck."

Susan was already there, dressed as an elf. "Can you believe this?" she cried, squeezing Lara's arm excitedly. "I was totally shocked!"

Christie played a tape and everyone danced. Barbie found Ken, who was dressed as a pirate. Together they danced out into the middle of the floor.

Everyone had a great time. All too soon it was nine o'clock, time for lights out. Barbie noticed that Lara looked worried. "You all right?" she asked.

"Just worried about tomorrow," Lara answered honestly.

"You'll be fine," Barbie assured her.

The next morning, Barbie awoke at dawn to get the horses ready to be loaded into the trailers. She hadn't been there fifteen minutes when Lara appeared, already dressed in a pair of denim overalls and riding boots. Barbie searched Lara's face for any signs of excitement, but saw none. "I know I'll mess up," Lara said tensely. "I always do."

"You're not going to mess up," Barbie said with gentle firmness. "You and Windswept have worked really hard to prepare for today."

"If we lose, it will because of me, not Windswept," said Lara glumly.

Barbie put her hand on Lara's shoulder. "The only people who lose are the ones who never try. I don't care about ribbons, Lara. I'm already proud of you for trying."

Lara and Barbie led the horses into their trailers. Midge had borrowed an extra trailer for Clover. As soon as they were finished, Midge and Susan joined them. Midge and Susan pulled Clover along behind Midge's car. Barbie and Lara followed them out of camp and down the road to the stadium, with Windswept in the trailer attached to Barbie's car.

When they arrived, the stadium was still almost empty. The audience wouldn't arrive for hours. Barbie helped Lara and Susan get the horses settled in their private stalls, then went off to get the girls their competition numbers. They would pin the felt numbers to their denim jackets when they rode.

"Here, Susan," Barbie smiled. "You're number eight. And Lara, you're number nine."

The girls turned and let Barbie pin the numbers to their jackets. "Let's take a look around," Barbie suggested. They walked around and came to a group of girls unloading their horses. Their horses' blankets bore the words "Chillborn Academy." The girls were all dressed in red velvet jackets with black collars, and black leather riding boots.

"They look so fancy," said Susan.

"Chillborn Academy is a pretty fancy place," Barbie admitted.

"Oh, well, we can beat 'em," Susan said. "Everyone routes for the underdogs. And I'd say that's us!"

"They've probably been riding all their lives," Lara muttered. "I bet they own their own horses. I don't stand a chance."

Barbie worried about the panicked look that swept across Lara's face. Sure enough, Lara turned and ran away from Susan and Barbie.

"Lara!" Barbie called, chasing after her. She was just in time to see the number nine on Lara's jacket disappear out the main gate.

9

The Good Luck Hat

Barbie glanced anxiously at a clock on the wall. The jumping competition would begin in fifteen minutes.

Barbie had to find Lara! On her way toward the front gate, she bumped into Kira, who was coming in with some campers. "Whoa, Barbie," said Kira. "Where are you going in such a hurry?"

"I'll explain later," said Barbie, hurrying past. She hoped she could find Lara and talk her into competing.

Outside, Barbie found Lara sitting on a log behind the stadium parking lot. She was crying. "Mind if I join you?" Barbie said quietly as she sat down next to Lara.

Lara wiped her eyes. "Have a seat. It's a free country."

"Lara, are you running away again?"

"No, I'm just not jumping," Lara replied.

"So you're quitting, walking out on all the people at Camp Lakewood who are depending on you?"

"It's no biggie," said Lara. "Everyone can cheer for Susan, She's a great horsewoman. She can win the trophy for Camp Lakewood."

Barbie took a deep breath. "Lara, I wasn't going to tell you this, because I didn't think you needed any added pressure. But there's a lot more at stake here than just a trophy."

"What do you mean, Barbie?"

Barbie poked at the dirt with a stick. "You already know that if you don't come back and ride Windswept, Midge is going to sell him. We really want to show her what a disciplined horse he's become."

Lara sat up tall and looked angry. She was about to say something, but Barbie raised a hand to stop her.

"And that's not all," Barbie continued. "What you don't know is that Midge needs the prize money from the competition to keep the horseback program at camp. If we don't win, the entire program will be disbanded."

Lara stood and dusted herself off. "She can't do that! This camp is one of the only places a kid like me can learn to ride a horse. Why should privileged kids be the only ones who get to ride? Windswept doesn't care what I'm wearing. He loves me for who I am."

Barbie smiled. "And so do I," she said. "But, just for luck, I want you to wear something special." Barbie took off her blue denim cowboy hat and handed it to Lara. "For luck," she said, crossing her fingers.

Lara smiled and put the hat on as they walked back inside the stadium.

As soon as they stepped in, they heard the booming voice of the announcer. "And now, the next to approach the hurdles is number nine,

Windswept, ridden by Lara Michaels of Camp Lakewood."

Cheers rang out from the Camp Lakewood section, but Lara was busy running toward Windswept. She passed Susan, who was just walking Clover back to her stall. "Hurry," Susan urged Lara as she raced past.

Midge took hold of Barbie's arm. "Is she going to be all right?"

"I think so," Barbie replied. "How did Susan do?"

"Wonderfully," Midge told her. "She did miss one jump, though."

Barbie watched as Lara rode Windswept out into the ring. The horse cantered toward the first hurdle, but Lara lost control of the reins.

Windswept was confused. He tried to jump the hurdle, but his hind legs hit the top bar. "Come on, Lara," Barbie whispered urgently from the first row of the bleachers. "Pay attention."

The shock of knocking over the rail seemed to jolt Lara to attention. She wiped the back of her hand across her brow and then brushed her hand along the rim of Barbie's hat. Then she looked over at Barbie in the bleachers and tipped the hat just a bit.

"That a girl, Lara," Barbie said quietly. "Be confident. You can do it."

The next thing Barbie saw was Windswept's speeding off at a gallop toward the next hurdle. Lara held on tightly as the horse leapt through the air.

One by one, Windswept cleared every hurdle—his body forming a magnificent black arc in the air. Through it all, Lara sat tall in the saddle, her chin held high with pride.

Barbie ran back to Windswept's stall to wait for Lara. "I'm proud of you," said Barbie.

"I didn't give up," Lara said proudly.

"You were terrific," Barbie told her.

"Let's hope the judges thought so," said Lara.

10

And the Winner Is...

"The judges will announce their decisions in a few minutes," the voice announced over the loudspeaker.

"What will we be judged on?" Susan asked as she stood waiting nervously with Barbie and Lara on either side.

"Lots of things," Barbie replied. "How you looked in the saddle, and how well you cleared the hurdles. The final scores will be flashed on the big scoreboard over there. The most you can get is ten points."

Finally, the judges announced their decisions. One by one, numbers flashed on the screen. Susan got an 8.8!

"Hey, that's the best score so far!" Lara congratulated Susan sincerely.

"Thanks," said Susan with a smile.

Lara's name flashed on the screen. And next to it was a 9! Lara had scored nine points out of ten!

Lara grabbed Barbie and gave her a big hug. "A nine! A nine!" she shouted gleefully. "Can you believe it, Barbie! Good old Windswept! I knew he could do it!"

The last score was flashed on the board. It was a 7.5. That made Lara the winner of the whole show, and Susan second.

Suddenly a big roar came from the Camp Lakewood cheering section. "Yeah! Camp Lakewood! We are number one! Yeah!" All the Camp Lakewood kids stood up and cheered.

At the awards ceremony, both Susan and Lara won trophies. And they each received checks made out to Camp Lakewood. From the center of the stadium, Lara waved her winning check in Barbie's direction.

Suddenly, the inside of the ring was covered with kids as the campers and counselors ran down onto the field. Singing "For they are jolly good fellows," the campers lifted Lara and Susan high on their shoulders. Barbie decided the horses needed a little celebration, too. She went back to their stalls and fed them sugar cubes. In a while, Susan and Lara came to the stalls. "What a great ending to a terrific summer," said Susan, clutching her trophy, a large, silver-plated cup.

Lara held her gold-plated cup and frowned. "Don't remind me that it's the end of the summer. I don't want to leave Windswept."

"Maybe you won't have to," Barbie said mysteriously.

"What do you mean?" asked Lara.

"It's something I'm working on," Barbie replied. "Now come on, let's get these horses back in the trailers."

"OK," said Susan, pulling her number off and tossing it into a trash can. Barbie noticed that

Lara folded her number neatly and put it in her pocket.

"You know, Barbie," Lara said as they drove back toward camp, pulling Windswept behind them in the trailer, "this is the first time in my life I've ever won anything."

"I think this is just the beginning for you, Lara," said Barbie. "I see a lot more winning in your future."

When they got back to camp, Barbie sent Lara and Susan back to their cabin to change. They had to get ready for the big end-of-camp barbecue. Ken and Alan had already set up a huge bonfire down by the lake.

At the farewell barbecue, Lara and Susan were surrounded by campers who wanted to hear what it was like to be in a real horseback riding competition.

"Next year, I want to learn to ride a horse," one of the youngest campers said to Susan.

"Well, because of the prize money, you'll be able to," Susan replied, smiling at Lara.

Midge came up and put her arm around Lara. "Thanks for saving the horseback riding program," she said.

"Thank you for giving me a chance," Lara answered. "I know I was a real pain for a while. I sure am going to miss Windswept."

Amy came up quietly behind Lara. "Maybe you won't have to miss him."

Lara looked at her godmother cautiously. "What's going on?" she asked.

"Barbie has been talking to your mother," Amy explained. "Your mom has agreed to let you stay up here with me for a while. You could take care of the horses and go to school in town. What do you say?"

Lara was so excited she couldn't do anything but smile at first. "I say that's cool!" she managed to yell at last.

Then it was time for a sing-along. One by one, the campers put their arms around one another and swayed back and forth as they sang their favorite camp songs to the tune of Alan's guitar.

"I guess you'll miss working with the horses, won't you, Barbie?" said Ken.

"I will, but I'll still be working with animals," Barbie told him. "I've volunteered to be the new head of the Sawyer Street Animal Shelter near my townhouse."

"Great idea," said Ken. "Need any help?"

"You can count me in," Christie said.

While the gang talked about the shelter, Lara climbed atop a picnic bench. "Excuse me everyone, but I'd like to say thanks to someone very special." She raised her cup of punch into the air. "Thank you, Barbie. You never gave up on Windswept—or me!"

Then everyone shouted at once: "Hurray for Barbie!"